Olive's First Sleepover

by ROBERTA BAKER

Illustrated by DEBBIE TILLEY

 LITTLE, BROWN AND COMPANY

New York ✦ Boston

For Isabel, with love and courage.
Dt 31:6.
—R.B.

For Gillian, love Mom
—D.T.

Little, Brown and Company

Hachette Book Group USA
1271 Avenue of the Americas, New York, NY 10020
Visit our Web site at www.lb-kids.com

First Edition: July 2007

Library of Congress Cataloging-in-Publication Data

Baker, Roberta.
Olive's first sleepover—by Roberta Baker ; illustrated by Debbie Tilley.— 1st ed.
p. cm.
Summary: Olive goes for a sleepover at her friend Lizard's house and, after she finds that
Lizard turns off all the lights to sleep, starts to worry about green ghouls and giant tarantulas.
ISBN-13: 978-0-316-73418-9   ISBN-10: 0-316-73418-7
[1. Sleepovers—Fiction. 2. Fear of the dark—Fiction.] I. Tilley, Debbie, ill. II. Title.
PZ7.B17485Oli 2006
[E]—dc22
2004026613

10 9 8 7 6 5 4 3 2 1

TWP

Printed in Singapore

The illustrations for this book were done in watercolor and ink.
The text was set in Fairfield and Providence, and the title was handlettered by Holly Dickens.

Olive Elizabeth Julia Jerome had played at Lizard Walinsky's house seventeen times before.

But tonight she was going to sleep over.

"We won't even need our pajamas," she hooted. "We're staying up all night!"

"Let's dress up as Madame Salamander and the Newt Princess and put on a show for my parents," Lizard chirped.

Before dark they collected caterpillars, slugs, and fireflies and charged the neighbors ten cents to pet them.

For dinner they played pizza parlor.

"How about pepperoni, marshmallow, and chocolate chip?"

"With strawberry sauce and pickles!"

"Don't you two eat anything normal?" Lizard's sister, Lulu, groaned.

Finally, when it was time for bed, they made a blanket tent in Lizard's room and built a tunnel out of pillows and toys. Olive arranged her supplies from home: three bubble wands, her bug-finder flashlight, and a kit for making purple slime. Then she dressed Gumbo, her polar bear, in his favorite pajamas and propped him at the door.

"I don't want anyone sneaking up on our secret sleepover club."

"I know what you mean," said Lizard.

Olive sat on the bed and looked around. Now that it was dark outside, Lizard's room began to look spooky. Everywhere Olive turned, sinister shadows seemed to move.

"Lizard, how many lights stay on when you go to sleep—one or two, or ALL OF THEM?"

"I don't sleep with any lights on. DO YOU?"

"Um . . . I sleep with one or two . . . or three."

"Mr. and Mrs. Walinsky, do you mind if I call my parents? I think they might be starting to miss me."

"Mom and **Dad**, were you ever a teensy bit nervous when you were sleeping at somebody else's ╌use?" Olive whispered.

"Of course we were," cooed Olive's mom. "Everyone feels that way the first time. Whenever you're ╌aid of the dark, sweetheart, just look outside at the stars."

"We're sending you a magic kiss, along with a polar bear hug," piped her dad.

Olive felt braver after that.

She skipped back to Lizard's room.

When Lizard went to brush her teeth, Olive checked under the bed.

She peeked into the closet and toy chest, too.

"Coast is clear, no monsters here. . . ."

Then a breeze ruffled Lizard's curtains, puffing them into dragon shapes.

Lizard's T. Rex skeleton began to sway and creak. Olive hurtled down the hall.

"Let's have a pillow fight, Lizard!"
Afterward they held a staring contest.
"If I do this any longer, Olive, my eyeballs will fall out."
"Eyeballs can't fall out, silly. They're stuck inside with glue."
"Lights out!" Lizard's dad came to say good night. "Flashlights, too."

Suddenly, Lizard's room was completely dark—darker than nighttime had ever seemed at Olive's house, and darker than the sky outside. Olive pulled back the curtains to count the stars, but the stars were covered with clouds.

"The darker the better," Lizard whispered. "I'm not scared, ARE YOU?"

"Not me," Olive squeaked.

"How about a ghost story?" Lulu leaned in the doorway, grinning through fake vampire teeth.

Olive snuggled into her sleeping bag, clutching her cardboard cutlass.
I'm glad Lizard is sleeping closer to the door, she thought. *If there is such
a thing as a slippery, green ghoul, it will eat her first.*

Tick . . . tick.

Lizard's alarm clock was noisy.

Drip . . . drip.

Rain trickled down the gutter.

Plink . . . plink . . .

What's that sound? Olive froze.

After they were dry and dressed for bed again, Mrs. Walinsky plugged in a night-light in Lizard's room.

"This is a lot less scary." Lizard curled around her stuffed woolly mammoth and closed her eyes.

Olive tiptoed to the window and pushed back the curtains. The clouds had melted and the sky was bright with flickering planes and stars, the same ones that glittered over Olive's house.

Olive crossed her fingers and tried to think.
"I brought three magic wands."
"MAGIC WANDS?"
"Come on, let's get my sleepover supplies!"
Olive scooped, Lizard scrubbed, and Lulu helped
squeeze sticky sponges. Olive turned on the faucet full
blast until the sink filled with soapy water.
Then she passed out her bubble wands.
"So long, purple slime!"
"No slippery, green ghoul will bother us now!"

"Were you girls telling scary stories tonight?" Lizard's mom arched her eyebrows.

"Just a little one," Lulu peeped.

"This is the stickiest sleepover I've ever seen." Lizard's dad shook his head.

"How will you ever clean this up?"

"Lulu, you're a sticky mess!" Lizard's mom stood in the doorway and gasped, "What have you done to this room?"

Purple slime dripped on the tiles. Foam spattered every washcloth and towel.

Olive wished she were asleep at home. "We heard this creepy dripping noise, Mrs. Walinsky. We . . . thought the slippery, green ghoul was coming. . . ."

"LET ME GO!" the monster bellowed.
Olive flicked on her bug-finder flashlight.
"You mean, you're not a tarantula?"
"Or a slippery, green ghoul?"
"Of course not, you silly mosquitoes!"

"Quick, grab the sheet!" They flung it over the monster's head, then tumbled together in a rolling heap. "GOTCHA!"

They huddled outside the bathroom door.

Tick . . . tick.

Drip . . . drip.

THWOP, THWOP . . . The sound of shuffling feet came from the darkest corner of
the hallway. The gray silhouette of something big stumbled toward the jump-rope web.

Olive's heart pounded. "Look! I think it's a spider."

"Not just any spider." Lizard froze. "A giant tarantula, the dangerous kind!!"

"Lizard, did you hear that?" she yelled in her loudest whisper.
"THE SLIPPERY, GREEN GHOUL IS IN YOUR HOUSE!"
"There's no such thing." Lizard rolled over. "Lulu was making that up."
"Wwell ssomething's here!" Olive sputtered. "You don't want to be monster
dinner, do you? WE'D BETTER CATCH IT BEFORE IT CATCHES US!"

They put on pirate hats and tiptoed down the hall.
"Are you *sure* you heard something?" Lizard whispered.
Drip . . . drip.
Plink . . . plink.
The sounds got louder with each step.

"Ouch!" Olive banged into the bathroom door.

"Look, it's only a drippy faucet." Lizard sighed with relief.

"Still, it was a very scary drip," said Olive. "I think we should set a trap just in case."

"I know! Monsters are attracted to things that are gooey," cheeped Lizard. "Let's get your purple slime!"

Together they laced Lizard's jump ropes across the bathroom door, lathered on Lulu's hairstyling foam, and painted Olive's slime in zigzag stripes to the floor.

"This is the stickiest trap I've ever seen. Let's add bubble bath for good luck!"

"It smells disgusting," chimed Lizard. "Just the way monsters like it."

"Hello, stars. It's me, remember? Olive
Elizabeth Julia Jerome. One of these days
I'll build a spaceship and visit. But right
now I need to ask you a favor. . . ."

"It's a little too bright in here." Olive
yawned. "Would you mind turning down
your lights? It's time to say good night."